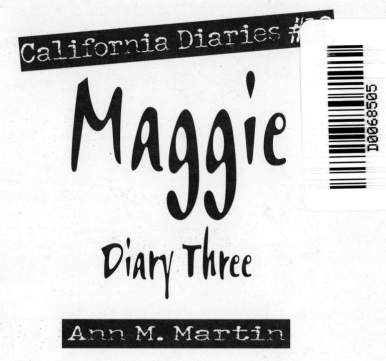

California Diaries #

Maggie

Diary Three

Ann M. Martin

SCHOLASTIC INC.
New York Toronto London Auckland Sydney
Mexico City New Delhi Hong Kong

*The author gratefully acknowledges
Jeanne Betancourt
for her help in
preparing this manuscript.*

ISBN 0-439-09547-6

12 11 10 9 8 7 6 5 4 3 2 1   9/9 0 1 2 3 4/0

Printed in the U.S.A.   40
First Scholastic printing, December 1999

I just read over this journal from the last few months and am reminded of all the intense things that have happened lately. The worst was Sunny's mother dying. It's been a whole month since Mrs. Winslow died and I still get teary thinking about it. She was so full of life and love. It's hard to believe that she's not around anymore.

I remember so many happy times at Sunny's house. Mrs. Winslow always came up with cool projects for us to do — like tie-dyeing or making veggie burgers before anyone else knew about them. We never said, "There's nothing to do," when we were at Sunny's.

We were four best friends then — Sunny, Dawn, Jill, and me. Of course, Jill isn't part of our group anymore. And for awhile I thought Sunny was going to go off in a different direction too. Now she's more like herself again. She's stopped running away from her problems.

I guess in the past few months I've stopped running away from my problems too. Or at least

I've stopped running from some of them. I look back at the entries where I wrote down everything that I ate — even a carrot stick. I kept writing that I was FAT FAT FAT. How could I not have realized that I had a problem? It seemed so normal to me then.

Now it's so strange. It seems like that was a long time ago.

I'm glad it seems that way.

I'm a lot better about food. My friends are a great help — especially Amalia and Ducky. And of course Dr. Fuentes. Being in therapy is like writing in a diary that talks back.

What surprises me the most is how much I've written about Justin lately. First I liked him and he didn't even notice me. When he finally did notice me and sort of liked me, all I could think about was not eating. Needless to say, he was not impressed. Now I'm better about eating, but Justin doesn't seem to be interested in me anymore.

Do I care?

I'm not sure. Especially after what happened in school today.

I was in a stall in the bathroom. I heard two

girls come in. They were talking about Justin, so I stayed in the stall and listened.

STALLED

GIRL IN SHINY BLACK BOOTS: Justin Randall is crazy about you, Nancy. You should have seen the way he looked at you when you came into math. You know it's true.

NANCY (brown loafers): Shhh.

BLACK BOOTS: Look, you're blushing.

NANCY (lowers voice): We're just friends. It's no big deal.

(Sound of flushing toilet drowns out rest of dialogue.)

BLACK BOOTS and NANCY exit bathroom.

Who's Nancy? Does Justin like her? Or is it really a "friend" thing?

I don't have a crush on Justin like I used to. But I felt sort of sick to my stomach when I heard he might have a new girlfriend.

Dad just came home. He's calling Zeke and me to come downstairs. Now!

I better go see what he wants.

Well, Dad's done it again. The big spender gives his kids the newest, the latest, the best.

Actually, what he gave us is pretty amazing. Zeke and I each now have a Handy palm computer. It really does fit in the palm of my hand. When I open the Handy, there's a tiny keyboard on one side and a screen on the other. I can also actually *write* on the little screen with this special pointer that converts my handwriting into type.

Dad said I should use the Handy for my address book, daily planner, assignment book, and to check my e-mail.

"Use it to take notes in your classes," he said. "Then download everything into your laptop later."

Right, Dad. I'm going to pull out this little techno wizard in class while everyone else is using pen and paper! It's bad enough I sometimes bring my laptop to school.

Zeke's already e-mailed three of his friends from his Handy. He can't wait to show his new high-tech toy to his buddies.

Really, I think the Handy is neat, but I don't want anyone at school to know I have it. It's embarrassing to have so much more stuff than my friends have.

"Only the best for the best," Dad said when he gave Zeke and me our Handys. "You can't be the best and the brightest without the latest technology. I want my kids to keep up."

I hate it when Dad talks like that. Why does he think money equals talent and brains? It doesn't. Period. Anyone with half a brain knows that.

Time to go.

10:00 P.M.

Well. Another typical Blume family dinner. Mom was drinking vodka and eyeing the wine bottle. Zeke was stuffing his face and talking a mile a minute about some *Star Trek* chat group on the Internet.

"Don't talk with your mouth full," my father boomed from the head of the table.

"Don't yell," my mother mumbled under her breath.

Dad steered the conversation to his new movie. He asked me, for about the twentieth time, if I'd read the script yet.

"I need a teenager's reaction," he said.

I reminded him that he only gave me the script last night and that I've been to school, done homework, and practiced the piano since then. But the truth is, I don't want to read *Love Conquers All.* It will be just as lame as his other movies. But I'll have to act like it's some big deal.

I haven't told any of my friends that Dad's landed Tyler Kendall for the lead of *Love Conquers All*. I'm not at all interested in "Hollywood's hot new teen star." I know what movie stars are like — especially the child star variety. Self-centered and shallow.

I tried to concentrate on my dinner. But with Dad's bragging and Mom's drinking, I could barely get down a few bites. I am always hungry before dinner, but when I sit down to eat with my family I lose my appetite. Now *there's* a diet.

I wonder if Sunny and her dad had dinner together.

Ducky probably picked up some takeout

tonight. Ducky — the most generous, sweet, lovable, fun guy in the world.

Dinner at Dawn's house will be a happy time, what with the new baby and all.

I bet there were extra people at Amalia's table. The Vargases are always inviting people to stay for dinner. It's so casual, homey, and fun at their house. I wonder if Brendan is eating with them tonight. Brendan and Amalia make a great pair, even if they're not fully ready to admit it.

Note to myself: Don't push the Amalia/Brendan thing. After James, Amalia needs to take her time with guys.

Note to myself #2: Springtime is a perfect time for new beginnings. I, Maggie Blume, do hereby resolve to have a great spring.

Me and my friends.

We all deserve it.

Wednesday 4/21
3:45 P.M.

Ducky and Sunny dropped me off at therapy on their way to Mr. Winslow's bookstore. Ducky had to be at work by four and Sunny was going too. She's been helping her father a lot. I think it does her good to be around her dad — and Ducky.

Since I'm fifteen minutes early for my shrink appointment, I'm typing on the Handy for the first time. I keep making mistakes on these little keys, but I think I'll get used to it.

I just wrote my schedule in the daily planner and copied it into my diary file. Cool.

4:00 P.M. Dr. Fuentes
5:00 P.M. Dinner at Amalia's
7:00 P.M. Vanish practice

What else do I have to report? Dad's big media campaign for *Love Conquers All* has started.

Why does everybody make such a big deal

out of movie stars? Dawn, Sunny, Amalia, and I were having lunch together when Jill and a couple of her new friends came over to our table.

"Tyler Kendall!" Jill shrieked. "He's going to be in your dad's movie? You could meet him? Maggie! He's only, like, the cutest guy in America!"

I explained about hairdressers, makeup, and touched-up photographs. "Besides, looks aren't everything. Especially if that's all you have," I concluded.

Sunny nudged my arm and grinned. "Come on, Mags," she teased. "Admit it. You'd love to be in the same room with Tyler Kendall and Felicia Hope. It's only normal."

I was glad to see Sunny smiling, but I wasn't crazy about what she was saying. My friends just don't believe how shallow movie stars can be.

"Felicia Hope is going to be in it too," gushed Jill.

"You'll probably meet them, Maggie," Dawn said. "I mean, you could if you wanted to."

I told her that I've already met Felicia Hope.

"You did?" exclaimed Jill. "That's so awesome. If I could meet Tyler Kendall I would die of happiness."

Jill pulled out a copy of *Stars and Hearts* magazine. Tyler Kendall was on the cover.

"Black hair and green eyes," sighed Jill. "And look at his smile. He's so perfect."

I told her that you don't know what's real and what's fake with actors. That he probably wears green contacts, has caps on all his teeth, and dyes his hair.

"That's an awful thing to say," spoke up one of Jill's friends. "How could you say that about Tyler?"

I love how they're on a first-name basis.

"Felicia is so beautiful," said the other girl with Jill. "He must be in love with her. I'm so jealous."

"She's totally fake," I said. "Including some of her body parts. And she definitely had a nose job."

"That's *so* not true," said Jill. "It's a rumor."

Amalia covered her mouth to stifle a laugh.

Jill and her friends begged me to ask Tyler to autograph their magazines.

I refused.

But Jill didn't give up. She left the magazine rolled up in my locker handle. A note was posted in the corner. "Please, Maggie. Just this once. I'll never ask you for a favor again. Love, Jill."

Hot-pink letters across the bottom of the magazine cover announced: TYLER KENDALL: EVERY GIRL'S DREAM BOY!

Not mine.

In Car. 4:50 P.M.

I have such a tight schedule today that I had our car pick me up at therapy and drive me to Amalia's.

My Handy is handy. So much easier to carry around than the laptop.

Key points from my session with Dr. Fuentes.

1. It's okay that I couldn't eat dinner last night. Admit to myself that eating with family affects me that way.

2. All people who like movie stars aren't shallow. And maybe some movie stars aren't shallow. (NOT MANY!)

3. Spring is a great time to have a great time.

4. Don't think so much. Just do.

Back from Vanish practice. Dinner at Amalia's was fun. I'm so much more relaxed there than at my own house. It's not that the Vargases are laid-back. They can be very intense. But they're intense in a good, honest way. Amalia's sister and her boyfriend had a disagreement about what they were going to do after dinner. But they talked it out honestly — instead of saying one thing and feeling another. WHICH IS EXACTLY WHAT DIDN'T HAPPEN BETWEEN ME AND JUSTIN AT VANISH PRACTICE.

When and I came into rehearsal, Patti was setting up her drums with Bruce. Rico asked me to play something while he adjusted the settings on the speakers. I took a quick look around to see if Justin was there.

He wasn't.

I sat at the piano and ran through a few numbers. I was singing "Friday Night Blues" when Justin came in.

"Wait back there!" Rico shouted to him. "You and Amalia listen from the back. Sing 'Touching,' Maggie."

I did.

TOUCHING
You came into my life
When I wasn't looking.

First, you touched me
With your eyes
And voice.
Then you put your hand in mine.

You came into my life
When I wasn't looking.

I see you now.
I hear your voice.
I hold your hand.

You came into my life.

It was hard to concentrate on the lyrics. I used to think about Justin when I sang that song. How could I want to hold his hand now? He doesn't want to hold mine. Does he hold Nancy's? I wondered.

I was very distracted.

After Rico straightened out the sound, Justin opened his guitar case. He didn't even look in my direction.

During the break, Amalia and I stood in the doorway, drinking sodas. After awhile, Justin joined us. Amalia said some normal, friendly things to Justin.

He said other normal, friendly things back to her. When he looked in my direction, I sort of smiled.

Rico called an end to the break and I headed back to the keyboard. Justin ran to catch up to me. "So how's it been going?" he asked.

"Fine," I said. "You?"

He beamed a huge smile. "Great. Things are just great."

Because of Nancy? Is that what he meant? Why did I have to say I was fine? Fine is such a lame word.

Why am I so nervous around Justin? It's not like anything big ever happened between us. We talked. Held hands.

Never even kissed.

I wish I knew about Nancy.

I'm sick of writing about Justin. I'm sick of thinking about him.

I guess I'll read *Love Conquers All* so my father will stop bugging me about it.

11:30 P.M.

Love Conquers All is a poor imitation of *Romeo and Juliet, She's All That,* and about a hundred other movies that were written a lot better.

Here's the plot in a nutshell:

Intellectual, nerdy schoolgirl is swept out to sea by an undertow while collecting mollusk specimens for a science project. Drop-dead-gorgeous surfer boy rescues her.

Surfer Boy and Brains go to the same school and are even in some of the same classes. She recognizes him when he saves her, but he's never even noticed her before. He mostly skips school anyway.

After the rescue he asks Brains her name. Embarrassed, she gives him a false one.

Back at school, Brains is lovesick and starts to question the way she's living her life. She makes friends with a hip girl who helps her change her style.

Meanwhile, Surfer Boy finally learns it's Brains he's fallen for. He assumes that she had given him a false name because she didn't want anything to do with him. He figures if he wants to get her attention, he better start attending classes and doing some work.

One day she cuts class to look for him at the beach (in her new beach bum look). But he's at school for a day of classes in the hope of seeing her.

They finally meet at the end of the day, through a totally unrealistic set of circumstances, and it's tru luv.

More stuff happens. His friends think he's nuts to like her, especially super-surfer Pam, who is after him.

Brains' father — principal of the high school — and mother — a scientist — are up in arms about the way she's behaving.

Our star-crossed lovers overcome obstacles and — SURPRISE! — live happily ever after.

Like that's real.

It's not any worse than any of Dad's other movies, so I'll tell him it's good. Meaning, good box office.

Which it is.

That's all he cares about anyway.

Friday 4/23
11:00 A.M.

Am using the Handy in the school library. Off in a corner where no one will see me.

When Zeke and I were having breakfast this morning, Mom came into the kitchen. This was a shock, since she NEVER gets up before we go to school.

Zeke asked her how it was going. He tries to act normal around her, but, like me, he's always wondering if she's been drinking. It was eight o'clock in the morning, so chances were good that she hadn't.

"Good morning," she said groggily. "You both look so sweet."

Zeke grinned at her. I felt pretty good too. It was nice to see Mom completely sober.

"Your father wants us to have a family dinner tonight," she announced. She stood up straighter and threw her shoulders back. "So be there."

Mom can do a great imitation of Dad.

"We already had a family dinner this week," I said. "What's up?"

"He must need us to do something for him," she concluded.

Of course she's right.

I wonder what he wants.

I hope I don't have to talk a lot about the script.

After Dinner, Before Homework

The family dinner is over. Fortunately, it didn't go on too long. Dad has a business meeting tonight so he left before dessert. Sometimes our family dinners are like a business meeting — with Dad in charge.

Dad announced the subject of tonight's "meeting" before Pilar served the first course. "We're having a party here next Friday for the cast and crew of *Love Conquers All*," he said. "It'll be a kick-off for the film."

"Couldn't you have it at that new restaurant in Santa Monica?" my mother suggested. "The one —"

"Eileen," Dad interrupted, "we have a big house so we can have parties like this. Besides, you won't have to lift a finger for this one. The studio is making the arrangements. Caterers and all. Even a piano player." He gave my mother a stern look. "All you have to do is pull yourself together and look good."

My mother turned from him and poured herself more wine.

I told Dad that I have a Vanish practice next

Friday night and asked if I could be a little late to the party.

Now Dad's stern look was directed at me. "I don't ask that much of you, Maggie," he said. "You can do this one thing without complaining — or sneaking out." He was remembering that I had sneaked out of the opening night party for his last movie.

"I wonder if Tyler Kendall and Felicia Hope have some romantic thing going," my mother said.

I shot her a grateful glance for changing the subject.

My father said he hoped Tyler and Felicia were romantically involved. It would be great for publicity.

I hope so too.

T.K. and F.H.

Two phonies in luv.

They deserve each other.

"Hey, Dad," Zeke put in. "Did Tyler Kendall drive his own car in *Protect and Serve*? Or was that a stuntman?"

"He's only fifteen," I said. "He's not old enough to have a driver's license."

"But they'd let him drive in a *movie*," Zeke said. "So did he, Dad?"

My father told Zeke that he didn't produce *Protect and Serve* so he didn't know. "You'll have a chance to ask Tyler that yourself," Dad answered.

"Cool!" Zeke exclaimed.

My father smiled at Zeke. At least one family member was excited about his party.

9:34 P.M.

Am going to call Amalia right now and tell her that I'll have to miss practice, and why. Don't want Justin to think it has anything to do with him.

10:00 P.M.

Amalia is too much! She thinks it's great that T.K. and F.H. are going to be at my house.

I reminded her that they are just movie stars and that there will be a lot of other people at the party. "Movie stars are in their own self-involved world," I told her. "They aren't normal."

"But Tyler was discovered just last year," Amalia argued. "He was an ordinary guy before that. Didn't he live on a farm or something?"

"Sure," I said. "In a town named Santa Claus. Santa Claus!"

Amalia laughed and said that Santa Claus, Indiana, was a real town and not a Disney kind of place with elves running around.

She's right, of course.

To get off the subject of Tyler, I brought up the subject of Brendan.

"I was just talking to him," she said. "He was the person on the other line when you called."

I said I was surprised that she hung up on him to talk to me.

"Of course I did," said Amalia. "Brendan understands. I'll call him back later."

Amalia's old boyfriend, James, would have had a fit if Amalia had interrupted a phone call with him to talk to someone else.

But not Brendan. He's a nice guy.

And Amalia is the best.

She's going to try to change next Friday's rehearsal to Thursday so I won't miss it.

Monday 4/26
3:30 P.M.

On my way to work at animal shelter. Stopped to buy fruit smoothies for Piper and me. Writing on my Handy. Getting used to the itty-bitty keyboard.

Sunny and Dawn were waiting for me by my locker this morning.

"We heard that you're having a party for Tyler Kendall," Dawn said.

Word sure does travel fast.

I explained that my father was having the party and it wasn't just for Tyler. Then I made them promise not to tell Jill. "And really," I added. "It's no big deal."

"Every girl in America is in love with Tyler Kendall," Dawn said. "And he's going to be at your house. Of course it's a big deal."

Sunny grinned at me. "So what are you going to wear?" she asked.

The bell rang for homeroom.

I told them Tyler Kendall is not going to notice or care what I wear. And that the only people who care how I'm dressed for these events are my parents.

Sunny was still smiling. "I'm on the case," she said. "Don't worry."

If helping me figure out what to wear makes her happy, I'll let her help me.

The truth is, I do need to buy something for the party. My size twos will be too tight on me now. And my clothes from last year are too loose. Besides, they aren't trendy enough. Dad likes me to look up-to-the-minute, fashion-wise. Mom does too.

I'm glad I'm going to the shelter. Dogs and cats don't care what your clothes look like or what size you wear.

6:30 P.M.

Mom and Dad are at some big benefit tonight, so Zeke and I had dinner in the kitchen. I told him about the two puppies that were dropped off at the shelter today. They are the cutest mutts I've ever seen. One is black with brown spots and the other is all black. I hope we find homes for them soon.

Pilar made a stir-fry with shrimp. It was yummy. I ate too much and feel stuffed. Tuna sandwich for lunch and the smoothie at work.

STOP IT, MAGGIE.

I have to stop keeping track of what I eat.

And not be so hard on myself if I do.

Ducky just called. He's going to drive me to the mall after school tomorrow and help me pick out my outfit for the party.

"You have to look smashing for that dinner, Maggie," he said. "And who better than Sunny and me to help?"

If Ducky had his way I'd wear foxy high heels and a glittery shirt to the party. Sunny's taste runs in the direction of short, tight skirts and halter tops. Still not my style. The problem is, I don't have a style.

"Sunny is so into this," Ducky said. "We have to do it."

"Of course," I agreed.

I better study.

Big math test tomorrow.

Going to the mall was a big production. A party of its own. Dawn and Amalia came with us.

Went to Ducky's favorite store first. Everything was glitter and retro. There was nothing in that store that I would wear to a Dad event or anywhere else. We had fun, though. Sunny bought a great-looking pair of shorts. I think it's the first time she's bought anything for herself since her mother died.

Next we went to Clarisse — this store Dawn loves. I tried on a couple of things. I kind of liked a shiny pink dress.

"It's okay," said Dawn.

"But not perfect," Sunny put in.

"And our Maggie has to look per-fect," Ducky declared.

As we left Clarisse I suggested that we

check out Rudolph's. "They carry Dana Lane dresses," I told my friends. "Those usually look okay on me."

"Dana Lane dresses are the *best*," Amalia said. "But Rudolph's is so —"

She stopped herself midsentence.

I know Amalia was about to say that Rudolph's is expensive. It is. And none of my friends can afford to shop there. I was embarrassed that I had brought it up. But it was too late. We were already walking into the shop.

The first thing I noticed was how quiet the store was and how noisy we were.

Ducky headed straight for the gowns.

Dawn threw herself on the white leather couch. "I'll supervise from here," she said.

Amalia took a deep breath. "It smells so wonderful in here. Like lilacs."

Sunny headed for a shelf with fancy hats. I hoped she wasn't going to start trying them on.

Ducky held up a shimmering black number and called, "This would look great on you, Maggie!"

A slender woman in a black suit came out from the back.

"Can I help you?" she asked in an icy voice.

Dawn jumped up from the couch.

Sunny pointed to me. "She needs a dress," she said. "For a party."

Ducky held up the black gown in front of me. "You have to try this on," he insisted.

"That gown costs two thousand dollars," the woman said as she took it from him.

Amalia gasped and Sunny giggled. Dawn was backing toward the door.

"A good gown like that is an investment," said Ducky. He was trying to act serious, but I could tell he was about to crack up.

"Perhaps you would find what you are looking for at Clarisse," said the salesperson. "It's across the way."

"We were just there," said Ducky. "No luck."

"We thought Rudolph's would have the perfect dress for Maggie to wear to this party for *Tyler Kendall* and *Felicia Hope*," Sunny said. "The party is at her house, so she has to look perfect."

"Per-fect," repeated Ducky.

The salesperson suddenly gave me a big phony smile. She knew who Tyler Kendall and

Felicia Hope were. And she'd finally recognized me. I had been there lots of times with my mother, who spends a fortune at Rudolph's.

"I'm sure we have the appropriate thing for you, Ms. Blume," she said. "I've just put out some new Dana Lane dresses." She looked me over. "I have one that would be perfect on you."

"Perfect is good," said Ducky.

I was pretty annoyed with the way the woman had treated us. I wanted to leave. But I saw that Sunny was having a terrific time. Now she could try on every hat in the store.

Sunny winked at me as she put on a big red hat. "Is it me?" she asked.

"Definitely," I said.

I followed Snobby Salesperson to the Dana Lane dress section.

I tried on a few things and we picked out a gray-green dress. Meanwhile, Dawn and Amalia each tried on a gown. They looked like princesses.

My dress is formfitting without being tight. And it has a neat neckline. I bought gold sandals to go with it. (Mom has since given my outfit her seal of approval. So that's taken care of.)

After I bought the dress and the sandals, we had pizza in the food court.

"Rhinestone earrings would go great with that dress," Dawn told me.

"And silver spangle bracelets," added Amalia. "I'll lend you mine."

I love Amalia's spangles. It'll be fun to wear them.

I told my friends I wished they could all come to the party.

"Me too," they said in unison.

I had to promise them that I'd tell them all about it. Even if I have a lousy time. Which I probably will.

Ducky did a wicked imitation of Snobby Salesperson morphing into Phony Sweet Salesperson. Sunny laughed so hard that tears rolled down her cheeks. She was having a great time. We were all having a great time.

It was when we were leaving the mall that my mood changed. I had noticed a couple kissing in front of the cineplex. The guy's face was blocked by the face of the girl he was kissing, but he looked familiar. Just then, the kiss broke up and he saw me staring at them.

I turned and ran to catch up with the others.

The guy was Justin. I recognized the girl too. Her name is Nancy Mercado. She's a freshman at Vista.

I didn't say anything to my friends about what I saw.

I'm glad I saw Justin and Nancy together. Now I know who she is and that she's his girlfriend. That's a lot better than not knowing.

I just wish Justin hadn't seen me see them. Ugh!

What's the big deal that I saw him kissing Nancy Mercado? It's a free country. It's not like he's my boyfriend. We hardly even talk.

So why do I feel weird about it?

Do I wish I were kissing him?

I wonder if the problem is that we never really broke up.

Or is it that we never really went out?

Why do I feel so awful about this? Why does it hurt so much?

I wish Amalia hadn't bothered to change the band rehearsal to Thursday. I don't want to see Justin. I wish that I didn't have to see him at school tomorrow either. But, of course, I will. We're always passing each other in the halls.

Wednesday 4/28

7:30 P.M.

Nancy Mercado came over to our table at lunch to talk to Amalia. Their families are friendly. Nancy was telling Amalia about her sister's baby shower. In the middle of a sentence, Nancy switched to Spanish. Amalia started speaking Spanish too. Suddenly, Nancy went back to English and apologized to Sunny, Dawn, and me. I guess she could tell by the expressions on our faces that we didn't understand what she and Amalia were saying.

When we were walking to our next class, Dawn said she thought Nancy was nice.

"She is," Amalia said.

Then I said I thought Nancy and Justin were going out.

Amalia said Nancy hadn't mentioned it to her.

"Maybe that was because Nancy knew that Justin and Maggie had a thing," Dawn suggested.

"But that's history," I said. "And it wasn't much of a thing anyway." Then I changed the subject.

Amalia gave me a look that said, *You just changed the subject.* But she let me get away with it.

I wish I could tell Amalia about the confused feelings I have for Justin. But I don't have the words to explain them.

I can't even explain it in my diary.

Thursday 4/29
3:30 P.M.

I'm so nervous about going to band rehearsal.

Justin will be there.

Are we going to ignore each other?

Won't everyone notice?

How can we go on being in the same band?

COUNTING
YOU...
Me...
And Nancy
Makes three.

Her plus you
Makes two.

One. Two. Three.
Was it ever you plus me?

One. Two.
What am I supposed to do?

One.

Rehearsal was way too weird.

When Amalia and I got to Rico's garage,
Justin was already in his usual spot, tuning up
his guitar. I thanked everyone for changing
practice for me.

Rico, Patti, and Bruce said things like, "No problem." Justin didn't even look up from his guitar. I knew then for sure that he had seen me seeing him kissing Nancy.

After going over our old material, we practiced a couple of new songs.

When Rico called a break, I stayed at the piano and waited to see where Justin would go. But he didn't budge either. I figured he was waiting to see where I went so he could continue to avoid me.

Meanwhile, Amalia and Rico huddled in a corner to go over some Vanish paperwork, and Patti and Bruce made a beeline for the snacks.

Justin fiddled with his guitar.

I finally stood up and made my way to the garage entrance, which was as far as I could be from Justin without leaving altogether.

I heard someone behind me. I turned around and found myself face-to-face with Justin.

He handed me a soda.

I took it, said thanks, and turned around again.

"How's it going?" he asked.

"Fine," I answered, without looking at him.

"Big party at your house tomorrow."

"Yeah," was all I replied.

I didn't say how I hate those parties. I don't know if I ever told Justin that. What did we talk about when we were "going out"?

"Maggie, I think I should explain," he said. "About Nancy. We're sort of —"

I put up my hand to stop him and said, "You don't have to explain anything to me. Really."

"But I want to. I was going to tell you, and then you saw —"

I faced him and made myself smile. "Justin, that's great. You and Nancy. She's terrific."

"I guess we're sort of going out," he said.

"Let's go, guys," Rico called. "We have a lot of material to cover."

"Coming!" I replied, then flashed Justin a parting smile, and went back into the garage ahead of him.

The first number we played after the break was "Touching." It killed me to have to sing it. I'd been thinking of Justin when I wrote it. Now all I could think was, it's true. Justin *was* kissing

Nancy. There's no romance between him and me anymore.

How am I supposed to pretend I have all these romantic feelings when I sing?

That was one unpleasant band practice.

And Dad's big party is tomorrow night. Argh!

I thought I was going to have fun this spring.

Friday 4/30
6:00 P.M.

Saw Justin and Nancy walking hand in hand in the hall today. Forced myself to smile as I passed them.

This would have been easier if Justin had told me about Nancy before I saw them kissing.

I think.

Have to get ready for the party. Raoul, Mom's hairdresser/makeup person, is here. Mom said he's going to do my hair and makeup too. I hate this.

Ducky just called. He pretended he was a French waiter who was working at the party and had lost the address. "So I'll be right over, zen, Meez Blume," he said with a fake French accent.

There's my phone again.

It was Sunny. She called to tell me to have fun tonight.

Asked me how my dress looked. I told her I didn't have it on yet.

"Well, put down the phone and put on the dress," she said. "I'll wait."

After I slipped the dress over my head I shouted toward the phone, "It's on. I'm putting on the shoes."

I picked up the phone and told her I was ready.

"How do you look?" Sunny asked.

"Okay." I checked myself out in the mirror. I looked good. How could I have thought I was fat back when I was a whole size smaller?

"Just okay? Okay isn't good enough."

"The dress is per-fect," I told her.

"Have fun tonight, Mags," she said. "You're so cool around all these big-deal people. I admire that."

I told her it was only because I know they aren't big deals.

"That's the other thing I admire about you."

That was really sweet. And I knew she meant it.

I'm so lucky to have great friends.

Just heard a limo pull up to the house. Time to make my appearance in the role of Hayden Blume's lovely daughter.

9:30 P.M.

What a boring party! And it's not over yet. Dad has taken everyone to the screening room to see scenes from movies that inspired him to produce *Love Conquers All*. I snuck up here to write in my journal. I want to remember what's happened so far, so I can tell my friends tomorrow. They'll want to hear every last detail.

The scriptwriters arrived first. Next the costume designer and her assistant. Then the director, Vance Vandersby, and his wife.

Vance is totally obnoxious. I noticed tonight that he pretends he's interested in you, but he's really looking past you to see who he should talk to next.

Dad calls that "working the room."

I call it "bad manners."

Vance was asking me about school, as if he cared, when someone called out, "Here they come."

Conversations stopped midsentence and everyone headed toward the front door. A white stretch limo was pulling up.

My dad jumped outside and opened the back door of the limo.

Felicia Hope stepped out. She was wearing a slinky, short hot-pink dress.

"Hayden, thanks so much," she gushed as she planted a kiss on Dad's cheek.

Next came Tyler. He had on black linen pants and a short-sleeved shirt with a black-and-gray checked print.

Dad and Tyler shook hands.

Dad looked around at the rest of us once they'd come inside. "You know everyone here," he said to Felicia and Tyler, "except my family."

Mom came forward. She seemed pretty sober. She kissed Felicia on the cheek and shook hands with Tyler.

Zeke was beside Dad now. Dad signaled me to join them. He put an arm around each of us.

"My daughter, Maggie," said Dad. "A musician, I might add."

Why does he do that!?

"And my son, Zeke. He's been looking forward to talking to you, Tyler, about your work in *Protect and Serve*."

Felicia gave me her big phony smile and said hi. I mumbled, "Nice to meet you." Felicia is only seventeen, but she looks and acts a lot older. She had on loads of makeup, spiked heels, and a "look at me" attitude.

Tyler said hi. He's fifteen and is really (I have to admit it) a good-looking guy. If green is the true color of his eyes. And if those waves in his hair are real. One thing is definitely real — his muscular build. I suppose he's been working out for this role. After all, he'll be wearing a bathing suit for a lot of his scenes. I wonder if he has to watch what he eats to keep that lean shape? Probably. Or maybe he's one of those people who can eat whatever he wants and still not gain weight. Like Justin.

The head waiter invited us to come around to the patio for cocktails. The piano player had arrived and was playing Broadway show tunes. I'd already asked Dad NOT to ask me to play the piano under any circumstances. And he had agreed. (Thank you, Dr. Fuentes, for helping me to say what I want — and don't want.)

Dad introduced me to more people.

I've met a lot of them at other parties, but I never remember their names. And I never know what to talk about, especially when they say things like, "You've certainly grown." Or, "Wow, Hayden. She's turning into a real beauty." Here's the comment I hate the most: "If she were my daughter I'd lock her up until she was eighteen."

I wanted to reply: "If you were my father I'd want *you* locked up until I was eighteen." But I kept quiet, still playing the part of the Good Daughter.

At dinner I sat between Felicia and one of the scriptwriters. Zeke was next to Tyler.

Tyler seemed to be talking — or listening — only to Zeke, who was showing him his Handy.

Vance and Felicia share the award for yakking the most during dinner. Even Dad couldn't outtalk them.

Vance was mostly talking about Dad and how great he is. No wonder Dad let him go on so long.

Felicia talked endlessly about her trip to some fancy Caribbean island, about the famous people she hung out with and the expensive restaurants and trendy bars they all went to.

"I told Tyler he should have come with us," Felicia said. She smiled at him. "You could have practiced your surfing for the movie, Ty."

Tyler looked up and smiled back at her. "Well, maybe I should have come," he said.

Dad looked from Felicia to Tyler. I know he was hoping their smiles were a sign that Tyler and Felicia are — or soon will be — romantically involved. You can't buy that kind of publicity.

Felicia suddenly turned to me. "Now tell me about you," she said. "How's school?"

"Okay," I answered.

She explained that she's been tutored since fifth grade and she wondered what it was like to go to a regular school. She asked me a lot of questions.

When she asked, "What goes on in the hallways?" I had a flash memory of Justin and Nancy walking hand in hand. I didn't include hand-holding in my answer.

But I did try to answer Felicia's questions as best I could. She was so interested and was really paying attention to what I said. I wondered if maybe I'd been wrong about her. Maybe she was a real person under that act. Maybe she wished she could lead a more normal life.

Dad overheard us and told Felicia, and anyone else who would listen, about Vanish and what a fabulous musician I was.

"How charming," said Felicia.

She smiled at everyone at the table and proudly announced, "Hayden's daughter is telling me about her school. I'm doing research for the film."

"That's our Felicia," Vance announced. "A true professional."

A true phony is more like it.

Felicia wasn't interested in me. She was just using me for research.

The screening will be over soon, so I better go back downstairs.

I won't tell my friends what happened next tonight. But I'm going to write about it. Otherwise I might not believe it happened at all.

After finishing that last entry in my journal, I left my room to return to the party. As I passed Zeke's room I heard a voice. But it wasn't Zeke's.

The door was halfway opened, so I peeked to see who was in there.

In the mirror over Zeke's bureau, I saw a reflection of Tyler standing in the corner of the room.

"How about it?" he was saying. "You said you'd do this for me. Are you going to?"

I was trying to figure out who Tyler was talking to. Then he looked up and saw me watching him in the mirror. He sort of waved.

I took a step into the room and looked around. No one else was in there.

"Sorry," Tyler said. "Zeke brought me up here. To see his turtles." He pointed to Zeus and Jupiter. "They're cute. I had turtles back home. I gave them to my brother Teddy, when I left. Teddy's Zeke's age."

I looked around the room again. "But where's Zeke?" I asked.

"He — um — went to the screening." Tyler was blushing with embarrassment. I was amazed. "Your father already showed me those film clips. When he signed me on for *Love Conquers All*. So I — uh — thought I could come up here to rehearse tomorrow's scene." He shrugged his shoulders. "I get really nervous before I start a new movie. Actually, I'm nervous all the way through the shoot."

I was caught off guard. He was being so honest.

"I'm a wreck whenever this band I'm in performs," I told him. "Everyone else is acting cool, but I'm a bundle of nerves. I can't hide it."

Tyler asked me what I did in the band. I told him I play the keyboard and sing.

"No wonder you have stage fright," he said. "You're singing in front of a live audience. That's scary and a lot harder than what I do."

"But there are all those people on the movie set when you act," I pointed out. "And millions of people are going to see the movie."

"Hey," he said with a laugh. "You're making me even more nervous. I need help!"

I couldn't believe it. He was asking me for help!

"Okay," I said. "What do you usually do to calm yourself down?"

"Rehearse. I feel like I'm a little more in control if I'm rehearsing."

I said it sounded like he was rehearsing the scene in which his character, J.B. (Surfer Boy), is trying to convince this studious guy, Tom, to tutor him so he can impress Vivian (Brains) in history class.

"You read the script?" Tyler asked.

I nodded.

"Do you like it?"

I was shocked. Why would Tyler Kendall want to know what I thought of the script?

"It's okay. What do *you* think of it?" I said diplomatically. "You're the one who has to be J.B."

"It's okay," he agreed. "But I have to find more to the character than what's on the page. That's my job."

"I'm sure you can," I said. And I was. I've seen Tyler in his other movies. He's good.

He tapped his hand nervously against his leg and said, "Thanks. I sure hope you're right."

Tyler looked so nervous I felt sorry for him. And before I knew it, I'd offered to help him rehearse.

I sat on the desk and he handed me the script. I read Tom's part. (I lowered my voice so I'd sound more like a guy.) Helping Tyler rehearse was really fun. He was nice — and normal. Not like Felicia.

He gave me the pages for another scene. It was the one in which J.B. rescues Vivian.

VIVIAN: You saved my life. I — I would have drowned if you hadn't pulled me out.

J.B.: You were really easy to save, you know. Maybe you could have even made it back by yourself.

VIVIAN: I couldn't. I can't swim.

J.B.: You're shivering. (Puts a towel around her shoulders.) There. That's better.

VIVIAN: Thank you.

When we were practicing that scene, Tyler used the blanket at the end of Zeke's bed for the towel. He gave my shoulders a little squeeze when he put it around them.

I looked up at him and our gaze locked for an instant.

"I'm glad I met you," he whispered.

I looked down at the script. That line wasn't there. He was saying it to me for real.

But was it real?

Or did he add the line so he'd understand his character better?

He is an actor, after all.

"Tyler, you up here?" someone called. It was Felicia. I dropped the blanket from around my shoulders as she came into the room. "What are you two doing, hiding away here?" She put her hands on Tyler's shoulders and cooed, "Everyone is looking for you, honey. They sent me to scout. I'm supposed to bring you back. Alive."

"Then let's go," he said, following her out of the room. He turned and winked at me. "Thanks, Maggie. For showing me the turtles."

"Turtles!" exclaimed Felicia. "How quaint."

Turtles?

Is that what the last fifteen minutes had been about for him?

Was I imagining that the time had been about something more than turtles?

I just don't know.

I looked around Zeke's empty room, like the walls could give me answers. But the walls weren't talking, so I went back downstairs myself. By the time I reached the living room,

Tyler was the center of a small circle of guests. He was Total Movie Star again.

Maura Davis, the assistant director of the film, started talking to me. She likes a lot of the same music that I like. I told her about Vanish and she told me all about a rock band she was in when she was my age.

I feel awful admitting this, but even as I was talking to Maura, I was thinking about Tyler. *He's an actor*, I told myself. *He turned on the charm. He isn't really glad he met me.*

People started to leave. The party was finally winding down. Maura asked for a tape of the band. I ran upstairs for it.

When I returned I noticed that Tyler was looking around the room. He spotted me and smiled.

"Maggie, thanks for rehearsing with me," he said. "It helped. I'm not so nervous anymore."

"Really? You're cured?"

"For now. Anyway, I'm really glad I met you." He smiled again.

It was like there was a current of energy running between us.

This is ridiculous.

He's a movie star.
I hate movie stars.

TO THE LAST STAR

Star light, star bright,
The last star I see tonight.
I wish I may, I wish I might
Forget the star I saw tonight.
Your light isn't real
And neither is the feel
Of your hand on my shoulder.
You don't mean
What you say.
They're lines from the script
You have to learn
So you can earn
A zillion dollars
Like my dad.
Star light, star bright,
The last star I see tonight.
I wish I may, I wish I might
Forget the star I saw tonight.

I want to forget Tyler. Did I ever have that buzzy, connected feeling with Justin?

Not like that.

Well, forget Tyler, Maggie. Every girl in America thinks she's in love with him.

YOU ARE NOT GOING TO BE ONE OF THEM.

Saturday 5/1
10:00 P.M.

Spent the day at the beach with Ducky, Sunny, Dawn, Amalia, and Brendan. We had a blast. It was so good to see Sunny surfing again. Sunny and Dawn wanted to know all about the party. I told them everything — except for the business with Tyler.

Had this weird moment at the beach today. This real cute surfer guy waved in my direction. I thought that it was J.B. Surfer Boy. *So* weird. That's the character Tyler plays, not Tyler. The guy waving wasn't J.B. or Tyler. It was a guy waving to someone walking along the beach behind me. What would have happened if it was

Tyler? Would he have liked my friends? Would they like him? Does he like me?

I have to stop thinking about Tyler.

THERE WAS A MESSAGE ON MY MACHINE FROM TYLER. Couldn't believe it. Here it is:

Maggie. It's Tyler. Listen, it was so great to meet you. I've been wondering if you'd come around the set sometime this week. We're shooting in Sound Studio 4. There's a lot of downtime on a movie. But of course you know that. Anyway, I thought it'd be a chance for us to talk. So I'll see you. I hope.

Guess I'll go. Of course I'll go. Tomorrow I'm working at the shelter after school. I'll go on Tuesday.

I'm crazy.

This is crazy.

Well, it's no big deal that he invited me.

But I'll just drop by to see the set. After all, it's my father's movie. Dad'll love it if I show some interest.

Tuesday 5/4

4:00 P.M.

Here I am on the set of *Love Conquers All*. I'm writing this while they're shooting a classroom scene. They'll probably shoot it a thousand times.

I haven't been on a movie set in ages. Five fancy trailers are lined up outside Sound Studio 4. One of them is Tyler's.

The studio is set up with a classroom, a school hallway, and a locker room. People are coming and going in all directions. There are extras dressed in hip "school" clothes and technicians working on the lighting and camera locations.

At first, I didn't see my father. Or Tyler.

As I walked around, a horrible thought

struck me. My father raised millions of dollars to make this movie with Tyler Kendall. Did Tyler invite me because I'm the producer's daughter?

I decided to leave.

As I turned around, Maura Davis called to me. She told me that she'd listened to the Vanish tape and thought it was great. Of course, I wondered if she said that because of Dad.

She also told me that Tyler was in his trailer. "He said to tell you that, if I saw you." She showed me which trailer was his and mentioned that Felicia had left for the day. "If you're looking for her."

"I'm not looking for anyone," I said casually. "I just dropped by, you know, because my dad likes me to." Meanwhile, I was glad that Tyler was looking for me and that Felicia wasn't there.

I decided to stop by Tyler's trailer on the way out. Only because Maura told me he was expecting me.

I was about to knock on the trailer door when it opened and a man came out. He had on a fancy suit and was carrying a briefcase.

I said hello and started to walk past him into the trailer.

He put out an arm to block me. "Whoa," he said. "Not so fast. No fans. No autographs. Let's go." He took my arm to lead me down the trailer steps.

I pulled my arm away. "I was invited here," I told him. "By Tyler. I'm Hayden Blume's daughter."

I have never, ever dropped my dad's name like that. I hated that I did it. I hope I never do it again.

But it worked.

The man's annoyed expression morphed into a big smile. He reminded me of the salesperson at Rudolph's.

"Nice to meet you, Ms. Blume," he said as he stepped aside. "Go right in."

I did. Without saying *thank you* or *excuse me* as I passed him.

I looked around the front room of the trailer. No one was there. So I followed the sound of rock music coming from the back of the trailer. It was an old Rolling Stones cut — a favorite of mine. I suddenly felt very bold. Tyler was just another guy. All the rest of it was show business — including the over-the-top fancy trailer.

"Tyler," I called. "It's me. Maggie."

I walked into the back room. Tyler was sitting at a desk with his back to me. He was reading a book.

When I called his name again, I startled him so that he almost fell off his chair. He steadied himself and turned around to face me.

"Sorry I scared you," I shouted.

He picked up a remote control and killed the music. "I was doing my history homework," he said shyly.

"It's not a real school out there," I kidded. "It's a movie set. The teachers are actors. You don't have to do homework."

He laughed and told me that he has to do schoolwork at least three hours a day when he's shooting a film.

I told him I was sorry to have interrupted him.

"Don't be," he said.

He invited me to sit down as he threw open the door of a minifridge. It was packed with juices, sodas, and snacks. "Do you want something to drink or eat?"

We each took a juice and sat facing each other in leather swivel chairs.

I told Tyler about the man who tried to keep me from coming in. Tyler told me he was his uncle and manager. "Uncle Fred loves being a big deal," Tyler explained. "He's my chaperone so my parents can stay home with my brother and sisters."

I asked Tyler about his family then. I could tell he misses them — and his friends. He said that they e-mail a lot, but it isn't the same as being there. And that every time one of his movies comes out, his friends start acting a little weird. Like they don't know what to say to him.

"They probably think I don't care anymore about how the S.C. High basketball team is doing and what's going on in their lives," he said sadly. "But I do." He motioned around the fancy trailer. "They'd be freaked if they saw all this."

"I know what you mean," I said. "Sometimes I'm embarrassed when kids come to my house for the first time. The house is so huge and we have so much stuff. And why? My dad makes movies. Big deal. A lot of people work even harder than he does and don't make enough to live on."

"Yeah," agreed Tyler. "I think, Who am I to make so much money and have all this attention? I'm not any better than anyone else. Just luckier. But I don't always feel so lucky."

"And you think, How can I complain about anything when I have so much? Right?"

"Right," said Tyler softly.

We looked into each other's eyes and I felt the current between us again — just like in Zeke's room.

"Tyler, put a move on," a gruff voice called out. "They want you on the set."

Tyler's uncle Fred stood in the doorway. "Of course you can come too, Ms. Blume," he told me.

Tyler said it would be great if I could come.

I said yes. I could tell he really wanted me there. Practically everyone Tyler deals with wants something from him. Tyler needs friends to talk to who don't want anything from him. I'm willing to be his friend.

But that's all.

Just friends.

Vance called a break, then they're going to shoot the scene — again. Tyler is headed in my direction. More later.

6:00 P.M.

Tyler talked to me during the break. We tried to carry on a conversation but were constantly interrupted. Makeup and wardrobe people were all over him with touch-ups and adjustments. Then the break was over. I knew they were going to shoot the same scene again. And again. So I told Tyler I was going to leave.

"Can you go out to dinner with me tonight?" he asked. "So we can talk some more? I could pick you up at seven."

Having dinner with Tyler seemed like the most natural thing in the world to do. I said *sure* without even thinking.

Now I can't believe it. I have a *date* with *Tyler*? Did I just write we're only friends? I meant that. Just friends. But I'm thrilled that we're going out to dinner, just the two of us. There's so much I don't know about him. I hope that he'll talk about his friends and his life back in Santa Claus.

I always worried about what to talk about with Justin.

With Tyler I'm not afraid about that at all.

I've been home for half an hour, but my parents aren't here yet.

I'll call Dad at work. I can't go out without telling at least one of my parents.

6:30 P.M.

Dad was in his office. I told him that Tyler asked me to have dinner with him. I explained that it isn't like a date-date, and that I think Tyler misses being around regular kids.

Dad said that was probably true. "But Tyler's in a strange world right now, Maggie," he said. "All this attention at such a young age. Going out with him isn't like going out with a boy from Vista."

I told Dad I knew that, but that Tyler wants to be treated like he's just another guy.

"Well, he seems to have his head on his shoulders," Dad conceded. "I'll say that for him."

I told Dad that I have my head on my shoulders too.

"I hope you do, Maggie. Because even going to dinner with someone as famous as Tyler can be a little bizarre. But go ahead. Have a good time."

It's a school night so I have to be home by ten.

I'm going very casual, in jeans. I don't want Tyler to think that I think our sort-of date is a big deal.

Now all I have to do is wait.

Just heard Mom coming up the stairs. Have to tell her what I'm doing.

7:00 P.M.

Mom's been drinking. Surprise. When I said I wanted to talk to her, she led me back downstairs to the bar. As she poured herself a drink, I told her that I was having dinner with Tyler and that Dad said it was okay.

She took a big sip of her drink and stared at me. "Are you crazy?" she exclaimed.

I told her it was just dinner and not a big deal.

"Avoid. Him. Like. The. Plague!" she said. She pounded the bar with her hand to emphasize every word. "Hollywood. Destroys. People." She took another gulp of her drink before continuing. "It destroys relationships. Show-biz people make lousy boyfriends, husbands, wives . . ."

She went on and on like that. Blah. Blah. Blah.

I couldn't stand listening to her. Finally, I just left the room.

I hate my mother.

There. I said it.

Well, maybe I don't hate her, but I hate the way she acts when she's drunk.

I hate that she gets drunk.

I hate . . .

I hate the word *hate.* And I don't want to

have all these negative thoughts before I see Tyler.

I'm going to go outside to wait for him. I don't want him to see my mom drunk.

10:15 P.M.

I don't know how Tyler puts up with it. It must be so awful to be in the public eye. I only had a little taste of what he goes through all the time.

Okay, Maggie, calm down and start at the beginning.

When the studio limo pulled up to the house, Tyler jumped out and held the door open for me. He was so sweet. I was glad I dressed casually, because he was in jeans too.

He said he was sorry he was late.

I told him he wasn't late and that I just felt like waiting outside.

Then he told me he thought we could go to this place he'd heard about, Fish 'N' Stuff.

On the way, he asked me questions about school and my friends. I knew he was asking because he wanted to know more about me. He wasn't doing research like Felicia.

When we were a couple of blocks from the restaurant, he told the driver to pull over.

"Do you mind if we walk from here?" he asked me.

I said it was fine with me. I do it all the time myself.

As we stepped out of the car, Tyler put on sunglasses and turned his baseball cap around so the visor shadowed his face. It was his disguise. We sat in a booth in the back of the restaurant.

No one but the waiter knew that Tyler Kendall was eating there. I like how waiters around here are very cool about that sort of thing.

We both ordered sodas and the fish of the day. I was so relaxed with Tyler that I had no trouble eating. We ate and talked and laughed. An hour and a half went by like ten minutes. I felt as though we could have sat there together for hours. But Tyler had to be on the set at six-thirty the next morning and I had my curfew.

Tyler put his cap and glasses back on. No

one in the restaurant even looked up as we walked past the other tables to the door.

We didn't see the crowd of reporters waiting for us until we were outside. Flashbulbs went off in our faces. Reporters pushed one another to get close to us.

"What's it like to go out with the cutest guy in America?" a woman yelled as she snapped my photo.

"Hey, girl, what's your name?" someone else shouted.

Another reporter stepped on my foot.

I was scared, but Tyler acted very calm. He said things like, "The shoot's going great." Then he put an arm around my shoulder and whispered into my ear, "Let's go." We moved quickly past the reporters. They followed us down the street, snapping pictures and shouting questions.

When we reached the corner, Tyler signaled to the limo driver. He zoomed over to us. We jumped in and slammed the door shut.

"Who is she?" I heard someone yell as the limo took off.

I was out of breath and felt like crying. Tyler

was breathless too. "I don't know how they knew where I was," he said.

I told him it was okay. But I didn't feel okay. Then I remembered this happens to Tyler all the time.

"I hate it when they trail me like that," he said as if he'd read my mind. "It's like I don't have my own life."

"So why do you do it?" I blurted out. "You can go back to Santa Claus."

"Because I love acting," he said quietly.

I felt sorry that I'd been so rude to him and said so.

"I'm the one who's sorry," he replied. "I asked you out for a quiet dinner and look what happened. It isn't fair to you."

"It's okay," I said softly. "It's over."

We were safe from the reporters. We were alone. There was no Felicia. No Uncle Fred. No makeup artists. No directors.

Tyler opened the roof and we leaned back and looked at the star-studded sky. We were sitting so close that we touched when the limo turned corners.

We didn't talk much. We just watched the

stars. I took a deep breath. I've never felt so happy.

When we pulled up in front of my house, Tyler asked me if I'd come by the shoot after school on Friday.

I said yes.

I can't wait to see him again.

Wednesday 5/5

12:30 P.M.

I've found a private spot in the library, behind the stacks, where no one will see me. If I'd known what was going to happen in school today I would have cut.

Jill was waiting for me at my locker. When she saw me, she started jumping up and down and squealing, like she was going to have a fit or something.

She held up a newspaper and shrieked, "How come you didn't tell me? I can't believe it."

Just then, Sunny and Dawn appeared. Sunny took the paper from Jill and looked at it.

"Maggie, you had a date with Tyler!" she exclaimed. "How come you didn't tell us?"

I remembered the reporters outside the restaurant.

"It just sort of happened," I said. "And it wasn't a —"

"Wow, Maggie," Dawn interrupted, "this picture. You look so — so surprised."

A small crowd was gathering around us. I felt as trapped and embarrassed as I had the night before with the reporters.

Amalia showed up and asked what was going on.

"I — uh — have to go," I mumbled.

Sunny thrust the newspaper in front of Amalia. "Didn't you see it?" she asked.

I looked down at the paper. There I was in living newspaper color, leaving the restaurant. I have a startled look on my face. Tyler, on the other hand, is smiling for the cameras.

"And look at this, Maggie," said Jill, pointing to the article. "Lana Brett wrote about you in her column."

Sunny read the part about Tyler and me out loud. By now a whole bunch of girls had gathered around us. Here's what Lana Brett wrote:

So where was America's number one teenage heartthrob last night? Not with **Felicia Hope**. And not in his swanky L.A. apartment rehearsing for tomorrow's big shoot of LOVE CONQUERS ALL. **Tyler Kendall** was on a date with **Maggie Blume**, the pretty daughter of the film's producer, **Hayden Blume**. They were seen leaving FISH 'N' STUFF at 9:30 last night. Tyler looked thrilled with his newest catch. But where does that leave his fabulous costar, Felicia? Out to sea? We'll keep an eye out for the next chapter in Tyler's adventures in the sea of luv.

I was so humiliated that tears sprang to my eyes.

The girls around me oohed and ahhed.

And then Justin showed up and asked what was going on.

Everyone suddenly became silent and Sunny put the paper behind her back.

"Nothing," Jill said between giggles.

Justin shook his head as if to say, *Girls can be so silly*. Then he walked away.

I grabbed my books, slammed my locker shut, and headed down the hall. Amalia, Dawn, and Sunny caught up with me and we walked to homeroom together. They tried to calm me down. But I was in shock and didn't even hear what anyone was saying anymore.

Why was Tyler so friendly to the reporters?

Maybe he likes the publicity.

I hate being the subject of a stupid gossip column.

I'm skipping the cafeteria. I can't deal with people right now.

Amalia just came into the library. She's looking all around. I suppose she's checking up on me.

1:15 P.M.

Amalia found me. I blew off some steam by telling her everything I was feeling.

"What am I doing with him?" I asked Amalia. "I hate movie stars!"

"You can't hate all of them," Amalia replied. "That's prejudiced."

"He seemed so real, Amalia," I confessed. "I mean, like a real person."

"Which he is," she reminded me.

Anyway, she said — and I know she's right — that Tyler didn't do anything wrong. It's not his fault he's so cute and popular.

I was going to cut the rest of my classes, but Amalia convinced me not to. If anybody mentions Tyler to me, I'm going to brush them off. I'll say, "He's just a friend. I don't want to talk about it."

That's the truth.

Amalia is a terrific friend. She invited me to dinner at her house. I *love* being at the Vargases'. More than being at home. I'm not nervous around Amalia's parents the way I am around my own. Is that awful to say?

3:30 P.M.

In the car, on way to therapy.

Checked my answering machine at home from car phone. Message from Tyler. He says he's sorry about the reporters and everything, that he had a good time with me, and would I still come to the set Friday. Wants to talk to me. Also said I might be right and that he should go back to his old life.

I'm upset about the stupid stuff in the paper. But I wouldn't want Tyler to give up his career because of something I said.

Time for Dr. Fuentes. More later.

Key points from my session with Dr. Fuentes:

1) It's not fair to blame Tyler for what happened.

2) My father's right that being famous can mess people up. But other things complicate people's lives too. Everyone has something. Sunny's mother died. Dawn's parents are divorced. Amalia had that awful experience with James. Ducky's parents are hardly ever home and his best friend tried to kill himself.

3) My mother is a bigger problem for me than I like to admit. I hate that she's so out of control with her drinking. Sometimes I feel like *I'm* the mother. (This is when I cried. I seem to cry about something in almost every session.)

4) Don't worry about Justin, since we both seem to be moving on to other people.

5) Relax. Take care of myself.

6) If I want to go to the set on Friday to see Tyler, I should go ahead and do it.

Friday 5/7

5:00 P.M.

Sound Studio 4. On *Love Conquers All* set.

When I arrived at the set about an hour ago, I walked around for a few minutes looking for Tyler. It seemed like EVERYONE was staring at me. I overheard a woman at the catering table tell the woman next to her, "That's her. The one in the newspaper."

Since I didn't see Tyler on the set, I headed for his trailer. He opened the door right away when I knocked.

I was glad he was alone, which meant we were alone.

"You okay?" he asked me.

I told him how people stared at me when I

walked through the set. "I don't know how you stand it," I said.

"Sorry. I still feel terrible about the other night."

I was just about to say that it wasn't his fault when the door to the trailer was flung open and Felicia walked in.

"Ah, the lovebirds," she teased.

"Cut it out, Felicia," Tyler said. "I told you we were just —" He stopped himself midsentence, then asked, "Wait — did you tip off the press?"

She grinned.

"*Not* cool," Tyler said. I could tell he was really angry. "I'd never do that to you."

"Publicity is good, Ty," she said as she flung an arm around his shoulder. "Don't be mad."

Tyler's uncle arrived then. A young woman wearing a headset and walkie-talkie was right behind him.

"We need Tyler and Felicia on the set," the woman announced.

"How are you today, Ms. Blume?" Uncle Fred asked.

I mumbled, "Fine," and left the trailer with everyone else.

They're filming on a new set now — a café/surfer shop called Catch the Wave. In the new scene, Vivian enters the café, nervously looks around for J.B., sees him, and shyly says hello. Then she has a line about surfing. He says something about school. They're each trying to make the other more relaxed. But they don't seem relaxed. Probably because neither of the actors are. They've filmed this scene six times so far.

I haven't had a chance to be alone with Tyler again. He came over to talk to me between takes. So did Felicia. I bet she was making sure we didn't have any more private moments. I think (I hope?) Tyler was as frustrated by that as I was.

Felicia is acting like she's jealous of me, which is way too weird to even contemplate. It's probably all an act, in case a gossip columnist shows up on the set.

Here comes the assistant director, Maura Davis.

More later.

Unbelievable.

Unreal.

Here's what happened.

Maura sat down next to me and said that she was glad I was there because she wanted to talk to me about something. Then she started telling me how Vance and my father have decided *Love Conquers All* needs a series of short takes of J.B. and Vivian having fun together. "You know, the look-how-much-they're-in-love scenes," Maura explained. "J.B. and Vivian picnic on the beach. He teaches her how to swim. They slow dance under the stars. Vance wants to have the dancing-under-the-stars scene on the deck of Catch the Wave. And he wants the music at the café to be live."

I wondered why she was telling me all this.

"I told Vance we should use a band with teen musicians," Maura continued. "I had the idea because of your tape." She said Vanish was the kind of band they'd want for that scene in the movie.

I was shocked and told her that I certainly didn't think we were good enough to perform in a movie.

She said that we were plenty good enough. She assured me it would be a short scene, and that our music would make it very authentic. "I thought you and your band would love the idea," she said.

I personally hated the idea, but I knew the rest of the band would love it.

"They love to perform," I admitted.

"We could also use some of your friends as extras," Maura added. "Say, fifteen of them. And of course you'll sing, Maggie. You have a marvelous voice."

Maura can't really think we're good enough for a movie. She probably had this idea because of Dad.

And my voice — well, what she said just isn't true.

Tyler joined us then, followed by Felicia. Maura told them the idea for the new scenes. And for using Vanish.

"A tape," Tyler said. "I didn't know you had a tape."

"Me neither," said Felicia.

Maura told them that Vanish was good and I was terrific.

I was blushing like crazy at that point. And my stomach was turning over.

"It's all so perfect," Felicia purred. "Maggie will sing while Tyler and I dance. It'll make a great press release."

Tyler glared at her. But she didn't pay any attention and flashed her toothy grin at all of us.

"I realize it's short notice," Maura told me. "But we'd love to shoot that scene while we still have the café set. Say, tomorrow afternoon. I can work out the details with your manager. Do you have a manager?"

I nodded and told her Amalia was our manager. I also told her I had a band rehearsal in a little while. Maura gave me her business card to give to Amalia.

"Have her call me as soon as possible," she said.

I looked at my watch. It was time to go. As I was leaving I heard Maura tell Tyler, "They're really good; I'll lend you the tape."

I'm so nervous. Tyler is going to hear me *sing*. What if he thinks I'm terrible?

I can't think about that. It's time to break my big news.

Everything is spinning out of control.

When I got to Rico's garage I motioned to Amalia that I had to talk to her privately.

We stood in the back of the garage. She asked what was up and I told her I'd just come from the set. I described the sequence of short scenes they were adding to the film. "They're going to show J.B. and Vivian having fun together as they fall in love," I explained.

"They do that a lot in movies," Amalia said. "But remember, Maggie, it's make-believe. Tyler doesn't like Felicia like that in real life."

I realized that Amalia thought I was jealous of Tyler and Felicia. So I blurted out the news that the director wanted to hire Vanish to play in one of those scenes.

"What!?" Amalia shrieked as she jumped up and down. "Maggie, you don't mean it! That is so awesome!"

I tried to shut her up. I wanted to talk about it quietly with her before anyone else knew. But it was too late. Rico, Bruce, and Patti ran to us to see what the commotion was all about. Justin followed, but he took his time.

Amalia told them the news. Everyone but Justin was excited.

"We'll be in the credits," Rico cheered. "In big letters!"

"Forget the credits, we'll be on the screen!" Bruce shouted. "Millions of zillions of people will hear OUR MUSIC! They'll see us!"

"What do they want us to play?" asked Patti.

"What should we wear?" added Rico.

I told them that Amalia was going to work out the details. I gave her Maura's card and she went into Rico's house to phone her. While Amalia was gone I told the band how boring it can be on a movie set and that they shoot a lot of scenes they never use.

But no one was paying much attention to

me. They were all too excited about the big break for Vanish.

Everyone but Justin.

"It's such a last-minute thing," he said. "How come?"

I explained that they had these new scenes to put in the film and they wanted to use a live high school band for one of them.

"And they heard our tape and they want us," added Rico.

"I just wondered," Justin continued. "I mean, whose idea was this?" He looked right at me. "Your father's?"

"Hey, man, who cares how it happened?" Rico said to Justin. "It happened and we better be ready for it."

"It wasn't my father's idea," I assured everyone. My voice was shaking, I was so embarrassed and angry that Justin had said that. "The assistant director for the film had our tape. I met her at that party for the film at my house."

"You meet a lot of people that way," Justin mumbled.

Had he seen the newspaper photo and gossip column?

Was he jealous?

Some nerve. I was nice to him about Nancy, so why was he being a creep to me about Tyler?

Justin didn't look at me again for the rest of the rehearsal. Or maybe he did and I didn't notice because I wasn't looking at him.

Amalia came back from phoning Maura. She told us we were performing two songs: "Rock It" and "You're Mine." "Rock It" is fast. But "You're Mine" is slow, so that must be the song that Tyler and Felicia will dance close to.

I'll have to remember that they are acting.

It's a movie.

Make-believe.

I'm so nervous about tomorrow that I couldn't eat a bite of my dinner. I know that's bad, but I couldn't help it.

Maura said the band should wear black pants and that the wardrobe department will have tops for them.

I have to bring three outfits I think would be suitable. Wardrobe will make the final decision about what I should wear.

Now I have to call Ducky, Dawn, and Sunny to tell them they can be in the movie if they want. Each of the other band members and Amalia are inviting two people so we'll have thirteen extras.

What if my friends don't like Tyler?

What if he doesn't like me when I'm with them?

What if I don't like him when he's with them?

What if . . .

A new thought — Justin and Tyler! Justin's been acting so weird toward me. How will he treat Tyler? How will he treat me when Tyler is around?

I have to worry about all of this and SINGING TOO!

Help!

10:15 P.M.

News and gossip travel faster than the speed of light around here. Ducky already heard about the shoot. Which meant so did Sunny and Dawn. They were waiting for me to call and officially invite them. Sunny thinks it will be a blast. Dawn loves the idea too.

But Ducky is way-over-the-top excited. He kept asking me what he should wear. I finally told him that his plaid shorts and Day-Glo green shirt would be perfect.

I didn't invite Jill to be an extra. I don't think I can trust her to act sane and calm on the set. But she'd be so excited if she could meet Tyler Kendall. It would mean so much to her.

I better invite her.

Otherwise, I'll feel guilty about it for the rest of my life.

I'll call her, then I'll go to bed.

I am so nervous.

How am I going to sleep tonight?

STAGE FRIGHT

Nerves.
On edge.
Stomach rumbles.

Fingers fumble.
As they stumble along the keyboard.
Voice croaks.
I choke on every word.
It's all gone wrong.
There is no song.

11:00 P.M.

Tyler just called. He was afraid he woke me up — which he didn't. He said he wanted me to know that he'd listened to the Vanish tape and loved it. He went on about how great my lyrics are. And said he loved my voice. I said thank you and stopped myself from saying I wasn't good. (Thank you, Dr. Fuentes!)

Then he said that I was lucky I can express myself through my music, especially by singing my own lyrics.

I said he expressed himself in acting.

"But I'm saying someone else's lines," he added.

We talked for quite awhile about that idea.

And other ideas too. I even told him how nervous I am about tomorrow.

I'm going to try to sleep now. Otherwise the circles under my eyes will be too dark for even Hollywood's best makeup artists to cover.

Saturday 5/8

Late

What a long, long, l-o-n-g day.

Ducky picked me and my three outfits up at 6:30 this morning. We had to be at Sound Studio 5 at 7:00 A.M. Sunny and Dawn were already in the car.

Sunny was wearing a tiny stretch top that showed off her belly button ring. She had her Rollerblades with her. I told her she was dressed perfectly for the scene.

"I brought some extra clothes," Ducky told us. "So the costume department will have some choices."

"I bet you have your whole closet in the trunk of the car," said Sunny.

We laughed. Ducky loves clothes. And he can never decide what to wear. So he probably did have his entire wardrobe with him.

Patti, Bruce, Rico, and their friends were in the sound studio when we arrived. They'd already discovered the catering table.

"Ho, Moggo," said Rico through a mouthful of doughnut. "Thos is gweat."

I looked around for Tyler. He wasn't there. Justin wasn't either.

Rico's father and Amalia went off for a meeting with Maura in the production office.

I spotted Justin, who had just arrived on the set. Nancy was with him.

I turned away so they wouldn't see me seeing them.

I wished Tyler were around. And then I wished he weren't. I was glad that Nancy was there for Justin. Then I wished she wasn't. I was so confused that a queasy feeling rippled through my stomach.

As I was opening a juice box, Jill whispered in my ear, "He's here, Maggie. He's here!"

I reminded Jill that she'd promised me she'd control herself on the set.

"But Tyler sees you, Maggie. And he's coming over HERE!"

I looked up. Tyler was headed in our direction. He gave me a hi sign.

I introduced Jill, who had the stupidest grin on her face. At least she didn't ask for his autograph.

It was weird introducing Tyler to my friends. Ducky was sort of jittery and nervous. He said something like, "Hey, Tyler, man, this is way cool, I mean such a big, fun thing for you to invite us, you know, to be in the movie and WOW!"

Sunny giggled.

Dawn acted like herself.

Justin totally avoided the being-introduced-to-Tyler moment.

Brendan, who'd arrived with Jill, was very laid-back and nice.

But I felt awkward and was relieved when Maura sent us all to makeup.

Tyler walked with me. Everyone left us alone for that couple of minutes. Except for Jill, who trailed us part of the way.

"I didn't think you'd be here until later," I told Tyler after Jill had faded away.

"I came early," he said. "To see you. And meet your friends."

Yes!

Tyler hung out with me while they did my makeup. I tried to carry on a normal conversation, but it was hard to do. Justin was in the makeup chair next to me. Tyler — who doesn't know that I used to have a crush on Justin — introduced himself. Justin was courteous but stiff.

I was also stiff. Or at least my face was. They put so much makeup on me!

After awhile, Tyler went to his trailer to do some homework. The rest of us went to wardrobe.

For the record, this is what we ended up wearing.

Rico, Bruce, Justin, and Patti: Black pants with tight, shiny polo shirts—hot pink (Rico), sage green (Justin), bright orange (Bruce), a gorgeous shade of blue (Patti).

Wardrobe wanted me to wear a black skirt with a shimmering silver sleeveless shirt. Dad came by, beaming, and gave me a big thumbs-up.

We rehearsed for an hour while the film crew adjusted lights, placed mikes, etc., etc. Maura said we sounded great. Vance said we're just what he wants for this scene. Dawn said my father came on the set when I was singing, but I didn't see him. I hope I didn't embarrass him.

Our Schedule:

1:00 P.M. Lunch break, Felicia and Tyler in makeup and costume.

1:45 P.M. Touch-up on our makeup on the set.

2:00 P.M. A run-through of the first part of the scene with Felicia and Tyler.

2:30 P.M. Cameras. Action. Take One.

I was so nervous at lunch I couldn't even swallow water.

While I was having my makeup touched up, I tried to swallow. I couldn't. My vocal cords were constricted.

When the makeup artist moved on to the next person, I made little coughing sounds to try to clear my throat. It was hopeless. I thought, I'll have to tell Maura I can't sing. I knew I'd disappoint the band members, but wasn't that better than ruining the scene by croaking?

"How's it going?" a voice behind me asked.

I turned and faced Tyler.

"I can't do it," I croaked. "Lost my voice."

"It's just stage fright," he said. "Remember?"

I shook my head no. "I can't sing," I insisted.

"Breathe with me," he said. "Slowly."

We took a few deep breaths together.

"Positions, everyone," a voice boomed.

Tyler smiled reassuringly at me and said I'd be great. He handed me a cough drop before he turned to go back to Felicia.

I unwrapped the cough drop, put it in my mouth, and joined the rest of the band.

I was still nervous. But more under-control nervous.

ESTABLISHING SHOT: Catch the Wave deck. Evening. Thirteen teens sitting at tables and standing around listening to a live band. Cool-looking boy and girl dancing on the side (Sunny and Ducky).

TRACKING LONG SHOT: Vivian and J.B. walk in and sit at a small table.

CLOSE ON J.B. and Vivian having intimate, silent conversation.

They did eleven takes of those three shots. We played the first chords of the song eleven times! In between the takes the crew made more adjustments to cameras, lights, sound.

We never played the song all the way through. They only needed the first stanza as background for those three shots.

By two o'clock I was totally exhausted and bored. And our music was beginning to show it. My friends, the extras, were dropping too. Jill had even stopped staring at Tyler.

Maura called a break. Vance went into a huddle with Tyler and Felicia to talk about the next scene. The rest of us threw back some sodas.

More makeup and hair touch-up.

Back on the set for the second half of the scene.

SOUND: Band playing love song. Lead singer at mike. (ME!)

MEDIUM CLOSE-UP: J.B. takes Vivian's hand. They stand to dance. J.B. puts his arms around Vivian's waist and they slow dance in place. She's tentative, he's more relaxed.

CLOSE ON J.B. whispering in Vivian's ear. She leans back and smiles shyly but lovingly. They dance even closer together.

FADE-OUT.

Tyler and Felicia did that LUV scene over and over and over. And I sang the same LUV lyrics for them over and over and over. All my friends were watching.

VERY WEIRD!

Finally, Maura shouted, "It's a wrap," and the shoot was over.

Maura thanked us and said it had been a great day. My friends seemed happy. Tyler said good-bye to everybody, told me he'd call me, and left with Felicia.

UNTITLED

I sang while you danced with her.
It was unreal.
What's the deal?
You pretend to be in love with her.
Is it an act?
Or fact?

Why did I write such a stupid poem?
I'm not in love with Tyler.
Tyler's just a friend.
I think.
I thought.
I don't know.
My friends were all happy about being
extras in a movie. They didn't even mention
how boring it was. Ducky thanked me about a
zillion times. Well, at least some people had fun.
Did Tyler?

Tyler called!

He said he *loved* listening to me sing yesterday. That it was fun to work together. He didn't mention that his "work" was holding Felicia in his arms and slow dancing.

It's going to be a crazy, busy week for him. They're filming the J.B.-saves-Vivian-from-the-undertow scene at some beach south of L.A.

"But I have Saturday off," he said. "Maybe we could double-date with Brendan and Amalia?"

A date? Well, he probably just means we'd go out with Brendan and Amalia. Hanging out with them will be a more normal way to see Tyler than on a film set. At least Felicia won't be there.

I told Tyler I'd check with Amalia and Brendan and get back to him.

Monday 5/10
1:00 P.M.

I'm in study hall and should be studying, and will study in a minute, but first I have to write what's on my mind.

Why is everyone flipping out about a little scene in a movie? The *Vista Voice* wants to interview me about the film. And someone from the student government asked if I could arrange a special screening of *Love Conquers All* as a fund-raiser for our library.

Do they think the movie is about Vista? Do they think Vanish are the stars of the movie? Just because we shot for a day doesn't mean our little scene will even be in the final film. It probably won't be. Movie producers spend millions of dollars shooting scenes that they never use.

Ducky acts like he had a big part in *Love Conquers All*. He'll be lucky if the back of his head is on the screen for a nanosecond.

This week I'm going to study hard, work at the shelter, and forget anything that has to do with movies.

Back to work!

Back to my real life!

Amalia and Brendan said okay to going out with Tyler and me Saturday night. Maybe we'll go bowling.

Will try not to think about Tyler until I see him on Saturday.

Wednesday 5/12

10:00 P.M.

It feels good to be back to my old routine. Lots of homework. Aced a math quiz with 100+. Going to work at the shelter after school tomorrow.

For the record: Dad said my singing on the set was "very good" and that Vanish has a "good sound." He also reminded me that a classical background in music is important and he wondered if I was practicing piano enough. He managed to turn a positive thing (that he liked my singing and the band) into a negative (that I wasn't practicing piano enough).

I hate it when he does that.

Talked with Tyler briefly. He's going to pick me up at seven on Saturday. We'll meet Brendan and Amalia at Alley Cat Bowling. Tyler said they finished shooting the rescue scene.

How many takes did they film of Tyler saving Felicia?

How many times did he give her mouth-to-mouth resuscitation?

Friday 5/14
8:30 P.M.

Phone message from Tyler.

Hi, Maggie. Sorry I missed you. I'm really looking forward to tomorrow night. My tutor is giving me a big history test tomorrow morning. Studying tonight. The shoot is going okay. Wondered how you're doing.

I heard Uncle Fred yelling something to Tyler in the background. Tyler signed off with a quick *Gotta go*.

Saturday 5/15
Sometime After Midnight

I should have known the evening would be a disaster. What was I doing hanging out with Tyler in the first place? I must have temporarily lost my mind.

Tyler picked me up at seven as planned. He talked about the shoot all the way to Alley Cat. He was pretty hyper from working all week.

When we reached the bowling alley, I reminded him to put on his sunglasses and hat. As soon as we walked inside, a guy Tyler knew called to him. His name was Rod Simon, and I figured he was a friend of Tyler's who happened to be there.

I waved to Amalia and Brendan, who were already at our lane. I was about to tell Tyler they were there, when two girls interrupted him.

They giggled a lot and asked for autographs. A couple of guys saw what was going on and wanted to talk to Tyler too.

I told Rod that it was nice meeting him and to tell Tyler I was going to our lane.

"Nice meeting you too, Maggie," Rod said. "See you over there."

I was a little surprised that Rod was planning to hang out with us, and I wondered if Tyler had invited him.

Amalia, Brendan, and I bowled a few practice sets until Tyler and Rod joined us.

Rod introduced himself to Amalia and Brendan. "Rod Simon," he said. "I'm following Tyler around for a few days. We're doing a lead piece on him for *Teen 'Zine*."

I was shocked. Tyler agreed to let a reporter join us!

I glared at him. But Amalia invited Rod to bowl with us. Brendan thought that was a great idea too. No one but me seemed upset that we were hanging out with a reporter.

But I was upset enough for all of us.

Actually I'm still furious. Tyler must have

suggested the evening because it would make good magazine copy.

Is that how he treats a date?

Is that how he treats a friend?

If it is, I don't want to be friends with him anymore. Especially since all he's interested in is being a superstar surrounded by adoring girls. He must have signed autographs for every girl at the alley. And even when he was bowling he'd look around and smile. He turned bowling into a performance and our evening into a publicity stunt. He's worse than Felicia.

I don't believe a word he said about missing his hometown and friends. I don't believe a word he says about liking to be with me. No wonder his friends in Santa Claus freak out about his being a star. He acts like one.

It was like Tyler wasn't with us.

Maybe he was wishing he was with Felicia.

Later, in the car, Brendan was telling us a story about his cousin who does bungee jumping. It was really interesting. Brendan asked Tyler if he'd ever done it and Tyler said, "Done what?"

He wasn't even listening!

Amalia made a joke out of it. And Brendan didn't act offended. But I was.

I should have trusted my instincts. I should have steered clear of Tyler.

From now on I will.

Monday 5/17
After Homework, Before Bed

Tyler left me an e-mail today. How did he get my e-mail address?

Maggie, I'm sorry about Saturday night. I was surprised that Rod showed up at the bowling alley, but I didn't want to be rude to him. He was just doing his job. But I know you didn't like having him there. I thought you might come to the set today. Or maybe you'll come later this week. Hope your week's going okay. Call me or e-mail back. Please. T.K.

I'm not e-mailing T.K.
Or calling him.
Or going on the set.

My rat brother gave Tyler my e-mail address! Zeke said he and Tyler have been e-mailing since the party.

Amalia says that Tyler really seemed to like being with us and that she could tell he liked me and wanted me to like him.

I said every girl in America is in love with him and shouldn't that be enough?

She said that he's not in love with every girl in America.

I said that was only because he's in love with himself, like every other actor.

She said I'm not being fair.

I said I had to go, that dinner was ready. Which was less rude than hanging up on her, which is what I felt like doing.

Wednesday, 5/19
8:00 P.M.

Talked a lot about Tyler in therapy today. I tried to imagine what it must be like for Tyler suddenly to find himself in that shallow, fake movie world. Everyone treats him like he's something special. I wonder if deep down he's thinking, *I'm just like everybody else. What's so special about me? Why is everyone giving me all this money and all this attention*?

Dr. Fuentes said that is often the way famous people feel.

I asked her if she thought I should give Tyler another chance.

She said I should do what I feel like doing.

8:09 P.M.

I feel like giving him another chance.

Later

Amalia said I should have a party and invite Tyler. She thinks he and I should be together without fans, reporters, directors, other stars, or any of the Hollywood hype. She says that'll give us a chance to figure out how we feel about each other.

So I'm having a party. A normal Saturday night party.

I'm going to go to the studio tomorrow to invite Tyler in person.

Maybe he won't come.

Maybe he'll be too busy.

Maybe he'll say he's too busy so he won't have to come.

Friday 5/21

As I was going up the steps to Tyler's trailer he came out. "Oh," he said with a surprised look. "Hi."

"Hi," I said back.

"I've been hoping that you'd show up."

We faced each other in the trailer doorway. I tried to look casual by leaning against the door jamb as I told him that I'd had a busy week.

He said that he wondered if maybe I was mad at him.

I admitted that I'd been a little ticked off about Rod Simon.

He apologized again for that. Then he said he was glad I was being honest with him. That he's sick of people saying one thing and meaning something else. "Which is the way Hollywood works most of the time," he added. He sounded much older than fifteen when he said that.

I told him about the party. He said it sounded great, and that although they were shooting tomorrow, he'd come right from the shoot.

When I asked him how the shoot was going, he said he was on his way to do another scene with Felicia.

"Which scene are you shooting?" I asked.

"The one in the library." He handed me his script and I quickly read over the scene. It takes place behind a stack of books.

Here's the dialogue (as well as I can remember it). A very romantic scene.

VIVIAN: No one wants us to be together. My parents, your friends, my friends. Nobody's on our side.

J.B.: Maybe you should stop worrying about this stuff. Let's just be together and see how we feel. This is about us. Not about them.

VIVIAN: But —

J.B. (putting a finger to her lips): Shhh. I'm happier when I'm with you than I am with anybody else, Vivian. That's the truth.

VIVIAN: I feel the same way.

Felicia caught up with us as we were walking to the set. She said hi to me, but all of her attention was on Tyler. "Don't forget that tonight after the shoot you're coming to my place for dinner," she reminded him.

"I know. And don't forget you promised we'll work on tomorrow's scene," he said pointedly.

I wonder if Tyler said that so I wouldn't think they were having some kind of big date.

"You staying for awhile?" Felicia asked me.

I told her no and said good-bye to both of them. I didn't feel like seeing Tyler and Felicia in luv with each other, even if it was acting.

Tyler looked disappointed that I was leaving. I guess that counts for something.

10:00 P.M.

Dad brought home selected dailies of the shoot with Vanish.

"I'm showing you the three best takes," he told me. "But we'll only be using a minute of that scene in the final movie — at the most. I hope you warned your friends."

The takes Vance and the editor selected are close-ups of Vivian and J.B. You barely see the band in the background. The camera is focused on the luv chemistry between Tyler and Felicia. All I could think was that they look the way I felt when that current was running between Tyler and me.

I must have looked pretty sad watching the

selects, because my father said, "They're only acting, Maggie."

I told him I didn't care. That Tyler wasn't my BOYfriend, just a friend.

"Which is all you should have at your age. Friends, and some of them happen to be boys. Know what I mean?"

Why do adults always say that?

Dad's knocking on my door to say good night.

Gotta go.

A Few Minutes Later

Dad came in with some suggestions for my party. He offered to have it catered by this fancy Mexican restaurant and hire a DJ. "Pilar can serve," he added.

I said I didn't want a DJ, fancy food, or Pilar serving us.

"I'm just trying to help, Maggie," he said.

I told him the biggest help would be if he left us alone. And made sure Mom did the same.

He put a hand on my shoulder.

"Don't worry about her," he said softly. "I'll take care of it."

I hate worrying about my mother being drunk in front of my friends.

But I'm glad Dad understands how I feel.

Saturday 5/22

7:30 P.M.

A party for eight that starts at eight.

Guests: Tyler, Amalia, Brendan, Sunny, Ducky, Dawn, Rico. And me.

I have a good supply of sodas, juices, pretzels, etc.

Pizzas are to be delivered at nine o'clock.

Since Zeke and Tyler have been e-mailing each other, I told Zeke he could drop in on the party as long as he didn't stay the whole time.

I'm very nervous about the party!

Tyler Kendall is an unreliable phony.

Why did I think he'd want to come to the party anyway? He probably only said he'd come to be courteous. He's probably at another party right now. Maybe at Felicia's. Later he'll have some brilliant excuse (A LIE) for why he never showed up here.

Why didn't he just come out and tell the truth in the first place? He says he loves the truth. He was probably afraid to say no to the producer's daughter.

I bet he and Felicia are laughing about how the producer's YOUNG daughter has a crush on him.

At 9:00, when Tyler was only an hour late, Dawn said we should wait for him to eat the pizza. I said, *absolutely not!* and served them as soon as they were delivered. We sat at the table by the pool, eating pizza and talking.

Ducky said that our lives over the past few months would make a good TV series.

"It certainly wouldn't be a sitcom though," said Amalia.

"If it's not a comedy then I don't want my character in it," Sunny told us.

No one said anything. But we were all thinking, *How can it be a comedy if your mother dies in it?*

"My mother would want it to be a happy series," Sunny said softly. "She loved to laugh."

Dawn reached out and gave Sunny's hand a squeeze. "You're right," she said.

"It'll be a sitcom with dramatic moments," Ducky explained.

"A comdram," suggested Dawn.

"A dramedy," added Amalia.

"Will I be in it?" asked Brendan.

"Yes," we shouted in unison.

Amalia and Brendan beamed smiles at each other.

We were all just fooling around about the TV show. But I was serious when I thought, *Tyler won't be in the story of my life.*

My friends are being very cool about the fact that Tyler isn't here. They've mostly ignored it and have had a good time without him.

But not Zeke!

"If you're having a party for Tyler, how

come he's not here?" he asked about twenty times. Finally he went to his room, but I had to promise him that I'd let him know as soon as Tyler showed up.

Now even Zeke has given up on Tyler. I just passed his room and he's sound asleep.

Sunny and Ducky are shouting for me to play water polo. I better go back to my own party.

After Midnight

Tyler finally showed up at ten-thirty. We were all in the pool.

"Hey, man, good to see you," Ducky shouted.

Brendan tossed Tyler a wet ball.

Tyler tossed it to me. "Sorry I'm late," he said.

I threw the ball to Dawn, but she didn't bother to catch it. Instead, she pulled herself out of the pool to greet Tyler.

So did Amalia and Brendan.

Amalia draped a towel over her shoulders

and talked to Tyler while Dawn went inside to zap the leftover pizza for him.

But I stayed in the water.

Ducky swam to the floating ball. He hurled it to me and shouted, "We might as well get out too."

I was the last one out of the pool.

Tyler was standing with my friends, acting like he hadn't been *two and a half* hours late for the party. "Sorry I'm so late," he said. "The shoot ran over, then this reporter stopped me, and —"

I put up a hand. "It's okay," I said. "It's no big deal."

"You're shivering," he said. He grabbed a towel from the chaise and wrapped it around my shoulders. "There. That's better."

I knew I was being unfair, but I still felt angry.

"You could have called," I said. My voice was tight. I was also angry at myself now. For making such a big deal about Tyler's being late. For caring that he was late. For caring so much that my stomach was in knots.

I asked who wanted ice cream.

Everyone shouted ME!

"I'm sorry I'm late, Maggie," Tyler said again as he followed me into the kitchen. "It was either this or not come at all. And I've been looking forward to this all day."

"Good," I said in a sort of friendly tone. "I'm glad you could come."

I opened the freezer and pulled out two boxes of ice-cream bars. He took them from me.

"I e-mailed my best friend in Santa Claus and told him about you," he said.

He was looking straight into my eyes. My anger and insecurity started to melt. I felt the warm current between us starting up again.

"I feel sorry for you, Tyler," I said. "It seems like you're working all the time."

"But being with you makes that okay. I'm happier with you than I am with anyone else."

That line was like a slap in the face.

I pulled back.

"What's wrong?" he asked.

"That's a line *right out of the script*," I said. "J.B. says it to Vivian in the library."

"Oops." Tyler blushed. "That happens when

I'm working on a film," he admitted. "I have to say lines so many times that they —"

"— come out too easily," I said.

"I was going to say that they become part of my subconscious."

I pointed to the boxes of ice cream bars and said that we should bring them to the others before they melted.

Half an hour later Tyler's limo came by to pick him up.

"Anyone want a ride?" he asked.

My friends all jumped at the chance to ride in the limo with him.

"You come too," Tyler suggested to me. "I'll drop you back here after we bring the others home."

"Come on, Maggie," begged Sunny.

"No, thanks," I said.

So my friends all left the party at once. And I'm alone in my room — wondering why I fell for Tyler when I knew better.

I wasted so much time thinking about him, hanging out at the set, getting Vanish involved . . .

Maybe I should have tried to work things out with Justin.

It's too late now. He has Nancy.

They're probably out having a great non-Hollywood time tonight. No one is following them around with cameras, asking them questions, and writing about them in gossip columns.

Starting tomorrow I'm concentrating on my own life.

A real life.

Without a script.

I'm going to forget Tyler Kendall ONCE AND FOR ALL.

Sunday 5/23

Two dozen roses arrived this morning. With this note:

For Maggie: Thanks for the party. Wish I hadn't missed the first part. Your friends are great. I have today off. Want to go to the beach? Call. Tyler

Sending expensive flowers after a party is such a Hollywood thing to do.

They're yellow roses. Yellow roses mean "I'm sorry."

I wonder if Tyler knows that?

He probably doesn't even know what color they are. Or even that they're roses. He probably told his assistant to send the producer's daughter a bunch of flowers.

I left a message on Tyler's voice mail. I said thanks for the flowers, and that I can't see him today because I'm working at the shelter. I didn't say anything about seeing him soon or that he should call back.

He's off the hook with the producer's daughter.

10:00 P.M.

Arrived at the shelter at noon.

My first job was to clean out the cat kennels. Piper said I seemed a little sad. She's super-sensitive and picks up silent signals from animals and people. Especially me. But she also respects my privacy. So all she said was, "If you want to talk about anything, I'm here. And if you don't, I'm here too."

I told her I'd be okay.

My next job was to take the two puppies out to play behind the shelter. The puppies are adorable. I hope they will be adopted together.

I was playing a game of chase with them when I saw someone running across the field toward me. Tyler.

He was breathless by the time he reached me. The puppies jumped on his legs. He bent over and picked one up in each arm.

The first thing he said was, "Look at these cute guys."

The puppy with brown spots licked his face. The black one nibbled on his jacket sleeve. Tyler laughed.

I couldn't help smiling. Tyler looked so happy with that armful of puppies. "Where'd they come from?" he asked.

I told him they'd been left at the door of the shelter in a cardboard box. "Where'd *you* come from?" I asked. "How'd you find me?"

"You told me about this place the first time

we went out," he said. "I remembered the name." He nodded to the black puppy. "This one reminds me of my dog, Coffee, when he was little. How many dogs do they have here?"

I told him that at the moment we had thirteen dogs and at least twenty-five cats.

"Do you like dogs better than cats?" he asked. "Or the other way around?"

"I know that a lot of people consider themselves either a cat person or a dog person. But I like both equally. I'm a both person."

"Me too," Tyler agreed. "We have loads of cats on the farm. And Coffee and a border collie who helps with the sheep." His smile faded. "I miss the farm."

"That must be hard," I said.

The black puppy snuggled deep into Tyler's arms and closed his eyes. The other puppy was now lying across my feet.

It was very peaceful in that sunny field with Tyler and the puppies.

"What's greatest about animals is that they don't care who you are," Tyler said. "If you take care of them and love them, they'll love you back. I wish people could be more like that."

I knew that what Tyler said wasn't from any script. It was from his heart.

I thought about how angry at him I'd been. I knew I'd been unfair. I'd judged him by his fame, not for himself.

"I'm sorry," I said. "For everything."

He inched closer. "Me too. Sometimes I wish I'd never come to Hollywood." He paused and looked deeply into my eyes. "But then I wouldn't have met you."

That's when he kissed me. It felt like the most natural thing in the world.

During the kiss the puppy in Tyler's arms licked the bottom of our chins. I giggled.

He put the puppy back on the ground and told him to find his own girlfriend. Then he put his arms around me and we kissed again.

Tyler helped me with the rest of my chores. I was impressed by how much he knows about animals.

"I want to be a veterinarian someday," he told me when we were feeding the cats.

"What about acting?"

"I'll do it for awhile longer, but it's not what I want to do for the rest of my life."

I told him that it was my dream to be a veterinarian too. But that other times I want to be a writer.

"You should be a singer too," he said. "You're a terrific singer."

I thanked him and said he was a terrific actor and maybe he shouldn't give it up so fast.

We said it would be great if we could do all the things we cared about.

It was interesting to talk to Tyler like that.

I've decided that Tyler Kendall is a great guy to know. It's not his fault that he's so famous.

I'll just have to learn to deal with it.

THE PUPPY

Yapping, jumping, loving, licking.
A puppy in your arms.
I was going to give you up,
But you held me close like that pup.
Understanding, forgiving, loving, true.
A puppy in your arms.
I was there too.

About the Author

ANN MATTHEWS MARTIN was born on August 12, 1955. She grew up in Princeton, NJ, with her parents and her younger sister, Jane.

Although Anne used to be a teacher and then an editor of children's books, she's now a full-time writer. She gets the ideas for her books from many different places. Some are based on personal experiences. Others are based on childhood memories and feelings. Many are written about contemporary problems or events.

All of Ann's characters are made up. But some of her characters are based on real people. Sometimes Anne names her characters after people she knows; other times she chooses names she likes.

In addition to California Diaries, Ann Martin has written many other books, including the Baby-sitters Club series. She has written twelve novels for young people, including *Missing Since Monday*, *With You or Without You*, *Slam Book*, and *Just a Summer Romance*.

Ann M. Martin does not live in California, though she does visit frequently. She lives in New York with her cats, Gussie, Woody, and Willy, and her dog, Sadie. Her hobbies are reading, sewing, and needlework — especially making clothes for children.

Look for #14

Amalia, Diary Three

I wish all of last night were a dream, Nbook. I could forget about it then. But it's stuck in my brain, and I can't stop thinking of those faces, those leering, harsh faces looking at me like I'm some thing, like an old shoe or a dead pigeon.

I don't look at anyone like that. Do I? No one's supposed to treat another person that way.

What did I do? What did I say? WHY DO I KEEP ASKING THAT?

I didn't do anything. I was there, that's all.